The Gull That Lost the Sea

By Claude Clayton Smith
Illustrated by Lucinda McQueen

For Adrian

A GOLDEN BOOK • NEW YORK

Western Publishing Company, Inc., Racine, Wisconsin

Once upon a sunny seashore there lived a gull named Gulliver.

Gulliver nested among the rocks below the lighthouse. His nest was made of dried seaweed, stems of grass, and old feathers. It was a very warm and wonderful nest.

The lighthouse rose above it like a giant peppermint stick.

Sometimes Gulliver hunted
shellfish on the beach. He
cracked open the hard shells
by dropping them on the rocks.

But most of the time he followed passing ships, feeding on scraps that fishermen tossed to him.

One day as Gulliver was following a tanker, dark clouds appeared on the horizon.

The wind grew stronger and the waves crested white.

Gulliver was tossed across the sky. The storm swept him inland over valleys and hills.

All night long the rain blew cold and sharp. But in the morning the sun returned.
Gulliver flew high above the countryside.

Instead of the rocky beach, Gulliver saw hills and fields. Instead of blue water, he saw green grass and trees. He could not find the lighthouse anywhere. Gulliver had lost his nest. He had lost the sea!

The warm sun dried his feathers, but Gulliver was
sad. He soared in wide and lonely circles.

Finally, far below, he spotted a village.
As he flew closer he saw...

... a lighthouse!

Well, it wasn't really a lighthouse, but it did look like a big peppermint stick, and it reminded Gulliver of home.

It stood in front of a little store called Tony's Barber Shop.

Tony looked out the window and saw Gulliver
sitting on top of his barber pole. Gulliver sat there
all day.

At closing time Tony threw
some pieces of bread out on the
sidewalk, and Gulliver flew right
down to eat.

The next thing Gulliver knew,
he was caught in a big net.

He was frightened at first, but then Tony picked
him up and he felt warm and safe.

Tony put Gulliver in a cardboard box. It had soft rags on the bottom and holes in the top to let in air.

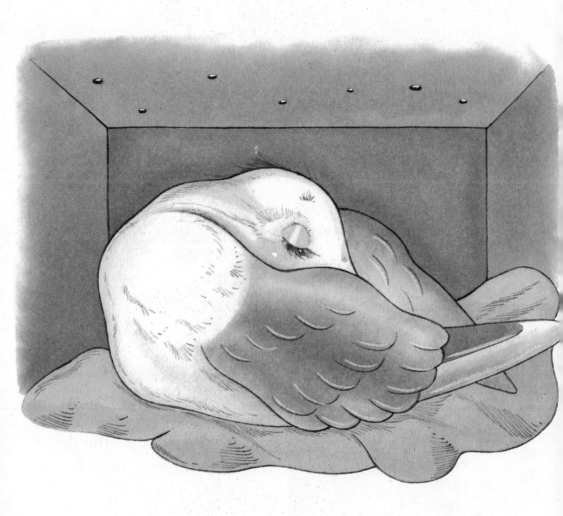

Gulliver settled down for a nice long nap.

SEASHORE

Next morning, Tony gave
the box to the bus driver.

SEASHORE

The bus traveled for a
long time across the
valleys and hills. At last
it stopped, and the driver
took the box outside.

When the bus driver opened the lid, Gulliver
flew up into the bright and sunny sky.

There was the rocky beach! And there was the
blue water!

And there was the lighthouse, tall and proud
above the waves!

And in the rocks below, there was Gulliver's nest, snug and warm and waiting.

Gulliver had found his home by the sea.